COCK-A-DOODLE-DOO!

Mudpuddle Farm

michael morpurgo

Cover illustrations by Cecilia Johannson
Interior illustrations by Shoo Rayner

HarperCollins *Children's Books*

For Anna

Mossop's Last Chance first published in Hardback by
A&C Black (Publishers) Limited 1983
First published in paperback by Collins, a division of HarperCollins, 1988

Albertine, Goose Queen first published in Hardback by
A&C Black (Publishers) Limited 1989
First published in paperback by Collins, a division of HarperCollins, 1990

This bind-up edition first published by HarperCollins *Children's Books* 2008

This edition produced for The Book People Ltd,
Hall Wood Avenue, Haydock, St Helens, WA11 9UL

HarperCollins *Children's Books* is a division of
HarperCollins*Publishers* Ltd
77-85 Fulham Palace Road, Hammersmith, London W6 8JB

The HarperCollins *Children's Books* website address is
www.harpercollinschildrensbooks.co.uk

1

ISBN 978-0-00-783529-4

Printed and bound in England by
Clays Ltd, St Ives plc

Mixed Sources
Product group from well-managed
forests and other controlled sources
www.fsc.org Cert no. SW-COC-1806
© 1996 Forest Stewardship Council

FSC is a non-profit international organisation established to promote the
responsible management of the world's forests. Products carrying the FSC
label are independently certified to assure consumers that they come
from forests that are managed to meet the social, economic and
ecological needs of present and future generations.

Find out more about HarperCollins and the environment at
www.harpercollins.co.uk/green

Contents

Chapter One

There was once a family of all sorts
of animals that lived in the
farmyard behind the tumble-down
barn on Mudpuddle Farm.

At first light every morning
Frederick, the flame-feathered
cockerel, lifted his eyes to the sun and
crowed and crowed, until the light
came on at old Farmer Rafferty's
bedroom window.

One... by one... the animals crept out... into the dawn... and stretched... and yawned. and scratched themselves;

but no one ever spoke a word, not until after breakfast.

SSSHHH

Mossop was a tired old farm cat who spent most of his day curled up asleep on the seat of Farmer Rafferty's tractor. Mossop paid no attention to Frederick – he got up when he pleased.

GUMLOP XL5

Farmer Rafferty was usually a kind man with smiling eyes, but like Mossop he was old and tired, and he ached in his bones in the wet weather. His animals were his only friends and his only family.

So, Frederick woke him up every morning.

Penelope and her speckled friends laid their eggs for him.

Auntie Grace and Primrose let
down their milk for him.

Upside and Down kept the pond
clear of weeds.

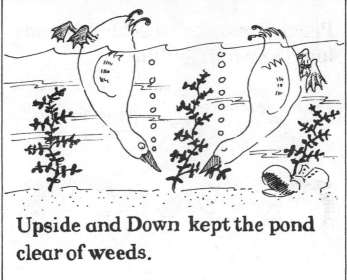

Captain carried him all around the farm to check the sheep.

Jigger, the almost-always-sensible
sheepdog, rounded up the sheep.

And Mossop was
supposed to catch
mice and rats.

Chapter Two

Farmer Rafferty always liked to sing as he worked. He sang in a crusty, croaky kind of voice.

la-la- tiddley-um-pom pom-tiddley-um-pom-pom-with-a-hey and a ho and a tiddle-iddle-po and-a-bing-bang-

Oh!

That morning though, as old Farmer Rafferty went into the tumble-down barn to fetch corn from the corn bin, he suddenly stopped singing.

The animals crowded into the barn
to find out what was the matter.
They found Farmer Rafferty
standing by the corn bin holding a
mouse up by its tail.

This is a mouse, and there are
three more in there, Mossop.

Mossop! Where is that Mossop?

Have we or have we not
got a cat on this farm?'
said Farmer Rafferty
in the nasty,
raspy voice
he kept for
special occasions.

'We have,' said
Auntie Grace, the
dreamy-eyed
brown cow.

'She's right,' said
her friend Primrose,
who always agreed
with her.
'We have, and
he's asleep on
the tractor seat.'

'Having a catnap,' sniggered Upside or Down – no one could ever tell which was which.

'Having his beauty sleep,' mumbled Egbert, the greedy, grumbly goat who ate anything and everything. 'Not that it'll help him much.'

'Fetch him,' ordered old Farmer Rafferty. 'Fetch that Mossop here. I have a thing or two to say to him.'

But at that very same moment Mossop wandered into the barn, yawning hugely.

MOSSOP!
Everywhere I go these days there's mice or there's rats. There's mice in my barley sacks, there's rats in my roof and now there's mice in my corn bin. I've warned you before and this time I have had enough. If you aren't up to the job, you will have to go. That's all there is to it.
Gulp!

Oh please, Mr Rafferty, Mossop does his best. He's just old that's all.

All right Captain, I'll give him one last chance to prove he's still cat enough to stay on this farm. Mossop, by tomorrow I want twenty-six mice dropped outside my backdoor, d'you hear me? Twenty-six mice or you're on your way.

Chapter Three

Mossop knew, and everyone knew,
that Farmer Rafferty always meant
what he said. So the whole day long
Mossop hunted

through the hay barns,

in amongst the barley sacks

and along the rafters.

But it was
no use, his
heart wasn't
in it.

He hadn't caught a mouse for a long
time now –

he was too old,

too blind,

too slow,
and he knew it.
Everyone knew it.

That evening, tired and miserable,
Mossop made his way back to his
sleeping seat on the tractor.

'How many did you catch, Mossop?'
asked Peggoty who lay surrounded
by her piglets on top of the steaming
dung heap.

Peggoty was a practical sort of a
pig. She could add up – which was
more than any of the others could.

'Catch anything, old son?' said
Jigger. Mossop shook his head.
'You've only got to say the word and
I'll give you a hand. Nothing would
give me greater pleasure.'

Captain's right, but thanks anyway Jigger. I'm too old.
Only got one eye and he doesn't work like he should.
And I'm slow as an old carthorse- begging your pardon, Captain. Anyway my claws are scarcely sharp enough to scratch myself.
As for my teeth- I've only got a few of them left and they're not much good anymore.

And all the animals – except one –
gathered round the tractor because
everyone loved Mossop.

But Albertine the goose sat on her
island in the middle of the pond,
and thought deep goosey thoughts.

Everyone agreed with Diana the silly sheep, which made her very happy.

'If Mossop can't see well enough,
then he should wear glasses,'
Auntie Grace said. 'That's what
Mr Rafferty does when he's reading.
He sees a lot better that way.'

But somehow that didn't seem to be
a good idea after all.

'If Mossop's claws aren't sharp
enough, we could sharpen them up
on Mr Rafferty's axe grinder,' said
Peggotty. 'Mr Rafferty's axe always
cuts better after it's been sharpened
doesn't it?'

But Mossop didn't think that
sounded much fun either.

Jigger said.
'Mossop could have false teeth like
Farmer Rafferty. After all, old
Farmer Rafferty always eats a lot
better when he's got them in. He
keeps them on the kitchen window
sill. I've seen them.'

So they all went off to look at
Farmer Rafferty's teeth.

But in the end they decided it
wouldn't be fair on Mr Rafferty to
take his false teeth, and anyway
they were far too big for Mossop.

Even Egbert the goat
tried to think, but he
found that a bit
difficult, so he ate a
paper sack instead.

Everyone thought . . . except Mossop,
who was far too tired to do
anything but sleep.

Chapter Four

Out on the island in the middle of
her pond Albertine sat all by
herself and thought deep, secret,
goosey thoughts.

She rose to her feet, flapped her
great white wings and honked until
everyone gathered at the water's
edge in high excitement.

When Captain had calmed them down, she spoke, and everyone listened. They knew that Albertine was a very clever goose.

Go to every mouse hole and every rat hole. Tell them all that they must come to the barn for a meeting.
But what if they won't come?
Just tell them that if they don't come there will soon be a new sharp-eyed, sharp-clawed cat on the farm. They'll come alright. You'll see.
What's it all about?
I don't know.
Good old Albertine.

Within minutes every mouse and every rat on the farm had gathered in the tumble-down barn.

Captain called the meeting to order, but the mice and rats all threatened to leave because Jigger was licking his lips.

Captain told Peggoty to sit on the dog's tail, just in case.

Albertine rose to speak.

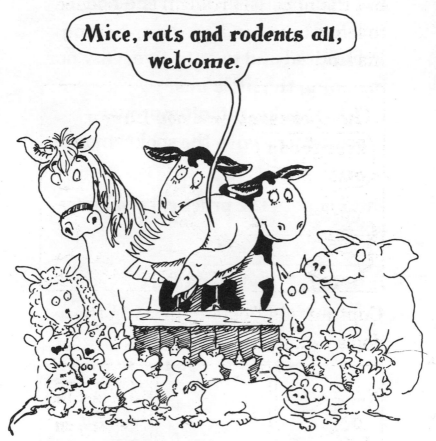

Mice, rats and rodents all, welcome.

And she told them her master plan.
They listened hard – except for one
little mouse who was playing chase
in the corner with Pintsize,
the tiniest piglet.

'How many of you are there?' asked
Albertine politely, when she had
finished.
'A hundred and twenty-five, Guv'nor,
including the little'uns,'
said the spokesrat, after proper
consultations with the spokesmouse.

But Peggoty the practical pig knew
better.

'Never mind. That will be quite
enough for what I have in mind,'
said Albertine, smiling.

Chapter Five

Mossop woke from his comfortable
dreams on the tractor seat and saw
the sun sinking through the trees.
He knew the time had come for him
to leave. Sadly he said goodbye to
all his old friends.

Everyone was there to see him off except for Upside and Down who never missed their tea, not for anything.

There were tears in Mossop's eyes as he crawled under the farmyard gate for the last time.

MUDPUDDLE FARM

Mossop! Oh Mossop. I nearly forgot. Farmer Rafferty says to be sure you go and see him before you leave just to say goodbye.
He won't shout at me again will he?

la-la-doobie-doobie-do-ho-ho-jingle-langa-dingle-dangle-o-la-la-la-la

'Of course he won't,' said Captain.
'He's happy again now. You can
hear him singing.'

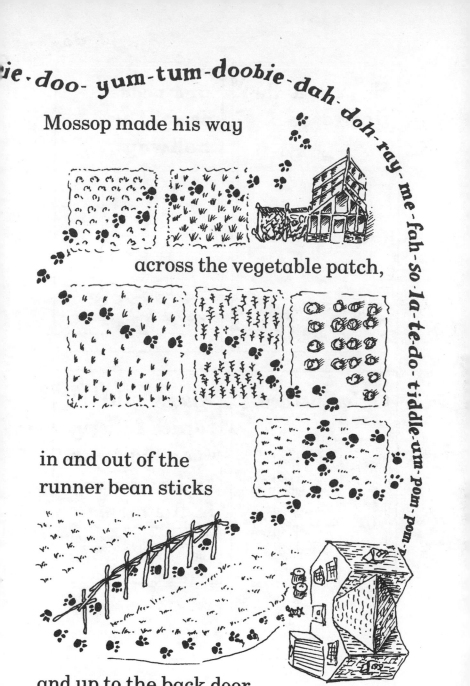

...ie·doo· yum·tum·doobie·dah·doh·ray·me·fah·so·la·te·do·tiddle·um·pom·pom...

Mossop made his way

across the vegetable patch,

in and out of the
runner bean sticks

and up to the back door.

He pushed the door open...

and padded down the hallway...

to the kitchen...

Where old Farmer Rafferty was sitting with his feet warming in the oven.

'Excuse me Mr. Rafferty, but
Captain says you wanted to see me
before I went,' said Mossop. 'I haven't
got any excuses Mr Rafferty.
I tried my best but I'm just not the
cat I was. It's age, Mr Rafferty,
old age. Well, I'll be on my way now.
Goodbye Mr Rafferty.

He took Mossop to the front doorstep, and there in front of his eyes, were row upon row of mice and rats.

They went right up to the goldfish pond and round and back again.

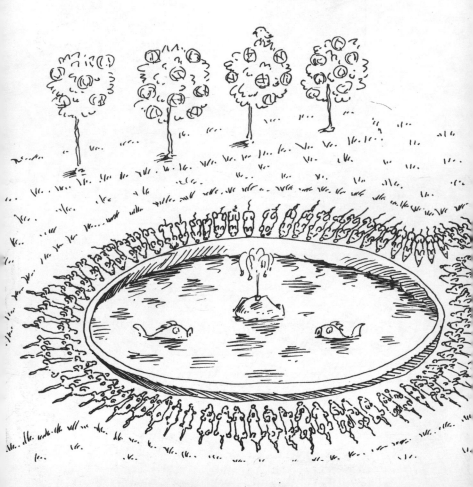

Mossop just stared and stared. He couldn't believe what he was seeing. Farmer Rafferty hung his old war medal around his neck.

My Military Medal, this is. Present from one old soldier to another, and I've no one else I'd rather give it to. You're a brave old cat and I'm proud of you. Off you go now, back to the farmyard.

Farmer Rafferty went back inside
the house shaking his head and
muttering to himself.

Then one by one they stole off into
the darkness until they were
all gone.

And he smiled as only cats can, yawned hugely, tucked his paws neatly under his medal, closed his eyes and slept.

The night came down, the moon came up, and everyone slept on Mudpuddle Farm.

Chapter One

There was once a family of all sorts
of animals that lived in the
farmyard behind the tumble-down
barn on Mudpuddle Farm.

cock-a-doodle-doo-be-doobie-doobie-doobie-

At first light every morning
Frederick, the flame-feathered
cockerel, lifted his eyes to the sun and
crowed and crowed until the light
came on in old Farmer Rafferty's
bedroom window.

One by one the animals crept out into the dawn and stretched and yawned and scratched themselves.

But no-one ever spoke a word, not until after breakfast.

Chapter Two

One morning, just after breakfast,
old Farmer Rafferty brought
Captain, the great black carthorse,
in from his field and led him into his
stable in the corner of the yard.

I'm shutting you in here, Captain.
The hunt will likely be
coming this way today and I don't
want you galloping out after them.
I'm shutting Jigger in the house as
well, otherwise he'll be running off
with the hounds. I'll let you both
out after they've gone.

And old Farmer Rafferty went out,
bolting the stable door behind him.

Captain pricked up his ears. In the
distance he could hear the hunting
horn and the baying of the foxhounds.

Soon all the animals in the
farmyard had heard it too and
were running for cover.

an tara ta diddle dum

Here they come!
You'd better get
inside, all of you.
They'll chase
anything
that moves.

Peggoty rounded up her little
pigs (not forgetting Pintsize, the
littlest of them all.)

lly ho! woof woof yap y

Auntie Grace and Primrose, the two
dreamy-eyed cows, made off
towards the barn door as fast as
they could go.

While Auntie Grace and Primrose were agreeing, Egbert, the greedy goat, Diana, the silly sheep, and Frederick, the flame-feathered cockerel, ran past them into the safety of the barn.

Aunty Grace and Primrose both decided to go in at the same time.

But Albertine the white goose
stayed just where she was, sitting
serenely on her island in the pond.

Howl Yap Woof Ya

What a fuss.

Upside and Down, the two white
ducks that no one could tell apart,
were upside-down in the water so
they couldn't see or hear
what was going on.

HUBBLE
BUBBLE

GLOOP
GLOOP

It's an outright liberty!

Yap
Yap

Yap

And Mossop, who had been fast asleep on the tractor seat, shinned up the tallest lime tree and hissed with terrible fury. He hated being woken up.

Chapter Three

The hounds came through the gate.
They came over the gate and round
the gate, noses glued to the ground,
tails swishing in the air.

Behind them came red-coated, red-faced huntsmen on snorting horses that tossed their heads and flashed their eyes.

Farmer Rafferty went in to shave.
He only shaved when he remembered
to, and he remembered to now.

FADE AWAY

Chapter Four

The animals crept out of the barn
and into the bright sunlight of the
yard. They did not notice the
panting pink tongue nor the pricked
up ears of the fox as he crawled
out of a bramble hedge smiling his
sneaky smile.

Here
we go!

But Albertine did.

'Good morning, dear friends,'
he said in his sneaky voice.

And all the animals jumped in their
skins and clung to each other in fear
and trembling.

Don't be frightened, dear friends.
I ask you, do I look as
if I'd hurt a hair on your head or a
feather on your back?
It's a hard life being a fox.
Not a friend in the world. No one to
talk to. No one to play with.

He sighed a sad and sneaky sigh.
Then he cast a long and horrible
sneaky look across the pond at
Albertine.

The animals hid behind each other and kept their distance. Only Pintsize was brave enough to step forward.

I'll play with you. I can chase my own tail and catch it quick as a twick, so I can easily catch you.

But Peggoty picked little Pintsize up by his ear and dropped him under Aunty Grace's legs with all her other little pigs.

The fox wiped a sneaky tear from
his eye.

Back home in my den, I have a wife
and five little babies, all of them
starving to death because I can't find
any food to take home to them.
Without food my babies will die.
Won't you help me, dear friends?
I beg you, think of my babies.

And all the animals thought of his babies and they could scarcely hold back their tears.

'A fox is a fox is a fox,' said Albertine
wisely from her island on the pond.
But no one was listening to her.

And they all agreed they would.

From his stable Captain could just see what was going and he whinnied his warning.

CAREFUL!
Don't listen to that fox.

The animals thought he was calling after the huntsmen's horses – but he wasn't.

Jigger, the always sensible sheepdog,
could smell the rank smell of fox
and barked loudly from inside old
Farmer Rafferty's house.

The animals thought he was calling
after the huntsmen's hounds – but
he wasn't.

'You are so kind, dear friends,' said the fox smiling his sneaky smile. 'I don't need much. Just some milk, a few eggs, barley, wheat, oats, anything you can find. And there's no need to hurry back. Take your time.'

So one by one the animals left the yard until only Albertine was left sitting on her island.

And Mossop of Course...

Don't forget the old Mossop who was watching everything from his branch high up in the lime tree.

And be sure you don't forget the sneaky fox who was padding slowly towards the pond, his tail whisking to and fro, his tongue sharpening his teeth.

Chapter Five

Mossop watched in horror from his branch as the fox tested the water with his front paw,

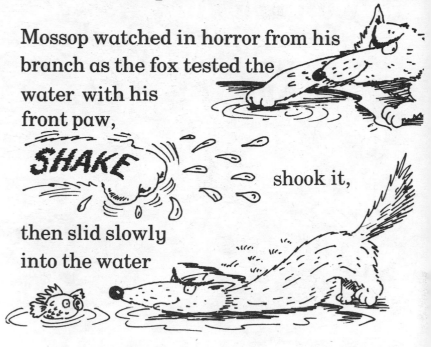

SHAKE shook it,

then slid slowly into the water

and swam out across the pond towards Albertine.

Who sat *still* as a statue.

Once on the island the fox shook himself dry and licked his lips.

But Albertine sat serene and still
and looked down her nose at the fox
as he came creeping towards her.

Completely unimpressed

'Mr Fox,' said Albertine, 'I am not
afraid to die. All of us have to die.
All of us have to die one day, you
know. Even you, Mr Fox. You can eat
me, but please, Mr Fox, take pity
on my children. Let them live.

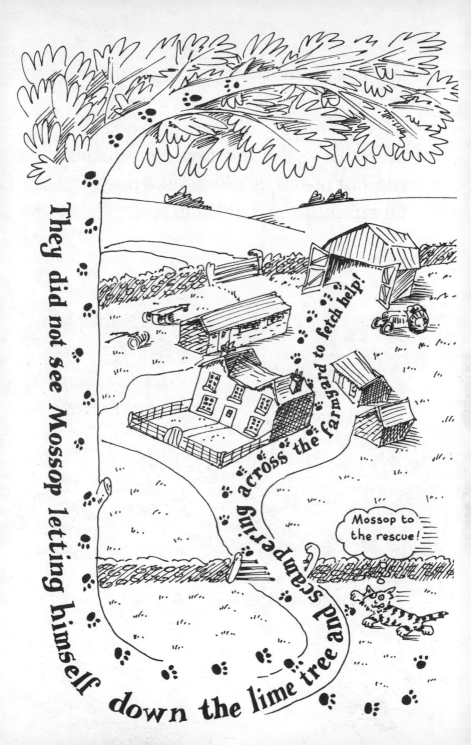

As Albertine spoke, she stood up
and three yellow goslings ran out
from under her feathers.

Chapter Six

The fox jumped back in surprise.

'You are brave, Madam,' he said in
a voice that was suddenly gentle
and kind, and not at all sneaky.

Five of the little perishers,
and they never stop eating.
You have three lovely children,
Madam, and they have a brave
mother. No, I just can't do it. I can't
kill you or your babies. Oh dear,
and I was so looking forward to a
nice fat goose - begging your pardon.

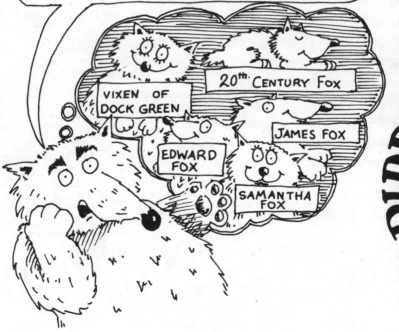

At that very moment the hunting
horn sounded. TARAN-TARA

Chapter Seven

There was a terrible baying of
hounds across the fields and the
drumming of horses' hooves.
The hunt was coming back . . .

The fox looked around him on the
island, but there was nowhere to
hide. It would take too long to swim
across the pond and he knew it.
He looked at Albertine with
pleading eyes.

Won't you help me?
I beg you,
please help me.

TARAN-TARA-TARAN-

'He's got to be here somewhere,' said the huntsman with the ginger beard.

And they all roared with laughter
and galloped off past the pond
and away.

But if the red-faced, red-coated
huntsmen had been in less of a
hurry they would have noticed that
the goose had suddenly grown

a long, red, bushy Tail!

Chapter Eight

By the time Mossop came running
back into the yard with the animals
behind him, they found Albertine
sitting quite alone on her island.

'Where is she?' asked Egbert, the
greedy goat, practising his butting.
'I'll get him, I'll get that fox.'

This
tale's
not
over
yet!

Even Auntie Grace (who was hardly ever angry) was lowering her head and pawing the ground like a bull.

Calm down dear!

And so, of course, Primrose did the same.

And Mossop hissed out his fury at the edge of the pond.

'I'm in here,' said the fox, as he crawled out from under Albertine's feathers, followed by three fluffy yellow goslings.

'Not me,' said the fox, shaking his head. 'Don't know what came over me. I'd better go before I change my mind.'

And he swam back across the pond and vanished over the hedge.

Chapter Nine

Later that afternoon

Upside ➡️

⬅️ and Down

at last

lifted
their
heads

out of the water.

'Had a good day?' Albertine enquired kindly, settled once again on her goslings.

'S'pose you've been sitting there all day doing nothing?' Upside sniggered, or was it Down - no one could tell the difference.

'You could say that,' Albertine said.

'Silly old goose,' said Upside, or
Down, and they both turned
upside-down again.

The night came down, the moon came up, and everyone slept on Mudpuddle Farm.